Paul Heyse

**At the Ghost Hour**

The Fair Abigail

Paul Heyse

**At the Ghost Hour**
*The Fair Abigail*

ISBN/EAN: 9783348096812

Printed in Europe, USA, Canada, Australia, Japan

Cover: Foto ©Andreas Hilbeck / pixelio.de

More available books at **www.hansebooks.com**

AT THE
GHOST
HOUR

THE
FAIR
ABIGAIL

TRANSLATED · FROM
THE · GERMAN · OF
PAUL · HEYSE
BY
FRANCES · A
VAN SANTFORD

WITH DECORATIONS BY
ALICE · C · MORSE

(((((** NEW YORK **)))))
DODD · MEAD · &
COMPANY
M · D · C · C · C · X · C · I · V

# THE FAIR ABIGAIL

HAT I have to relate lies far behind me in the past, remote by more than ten years. Yet at the slightest effort of recollection every detail rises before me as vividly as though it had all happened but yesterday; and I struggle against the same paroxysm of horror, that sensation as though my blood were **mingled** fire and frost, which overcame me upon that first dreadful night.

It was in the year of 1880, at midsummer. I had obtained from my superior officer a **few** weeks leave of absence, as my rheumatism had begun **to** trouble me about **that time.** The baths, upon which **I had** staked my hopes, did wonders for me. At the **end** of three weeks, I felt myself a new creature; and as the heat **of** that sheltered valley was likely to prove far from beneficial to me, my physician released me after the twenty-first bath, and advised me to pass the rest of my holiday **in** a cooler region.

Now, there was living in B— a friend **of** my youth whom I had not met since peace was restored. At the termination of the war, during which he had served as surgeon in my company, he **had** returned to this, **his native town, had** undertaken the direction of **its hospital,**

6

had married, and only announcements
of the births of his five or six children
had served to spin out the thread of our
old friendship.

As I came upon him now unexpectedly, it was the more delightful to me
to find him the same good comrade,
hearty and cordial, as when I took leave
of him, and received my discharge

from the list of wounded at Mainz.
Nothing would do but I must stay
and dine with him—the only
hour of the day, his amia-
ble wife said,
teasingly, when
he did not be-
long more to
the first comer

7

than to his own flesh and blood—
and as his practice kept him in de-
mand for the rest of the day, we
agreed that I should meet him after
the theatre, at a café which he desig-
nated.

My solitary afternoon passed quickly
enough. To
be sure, aside
from my old
army comrade
I didn't
know a
living
soul in
the beautiful old city. But there was
at every turn and corner, so much
of interest to see, there were so many
things to charm me and to jot down in
my sketch book, and withal, the air was
so delightful, cooled as it had been by
the morning's thunderstorm, that I
gave up the idea of attending the theatre—always a questionable boon in

8

summer, and chose to fill
up the time with a
stroll along the river-
bank in the still
evening air.

I had become
so absorbed in my meditations that
the thought of returning did not occur
to me until night was actually upon
me — a night indeed as delightful
with stray breezes as the day had been;
for the moon was rising
full-orbed and
lustrous over
the tops of the
alders, and so il-
lumined the country about that the
very pebbles on the level beach shim-
mered through the waves like little
silver balls.

The city, too, as I neared it, appeared
wrapped in a silver mist, as though
transplanted from some fairy tale. It
was striking nine from the old cathe-

9

dral tower; I was tired and thirsty after my long excursion, and sought well-earned rest in the café to which an obliging citizen directed me. As my friend had not yet come, I ordered something to eat and a pint of light wine to quench my thirst. And still the doctor kept me waiting. However, he was likely to come at any moment, and so I ordered in advance a fiery concoction of which he had spoken at dinner, that I might be ready to drink his welcome in this noble beverage as soon as he appeared. It was indeed "a draught of sweet refreshment" worthy to revive the bloom of an old friendship. Still he failed of his appointment, and towards ten there appeared, instead of my good comrade, a card on which my friend begged I would pardon his absence; but he had been summoned into the country to visit a patient who was seriously ill, and he could not tell whether he should return at all that night.

So, I was thrown back upon my own company, and upon the wine which,

unfortunately, was wont to lose for me its cheerful flavor, when not drunk in friendly company. Since I had lost my wife, nearly three years before, the flagon, unshared, gave rise only to a feeling of deep melancholy, which I was no longer either young or sentimental enough to nourish voluntarily. To escape it on this occasion, I seized upon the newspapers which lay plentifully at hand, as the few habitués were engrossed in scat or chess-parties at separate tables.

What first met my eye —upon the last page of the local sheet—was a list of the sights worth seeing in the town. As it was my purpose to remain a day longer, this guide was exactly what I wanted, and I noted down in my memorandum several things which excited my curiosity. Then my glance fell upon an advertisement which suddenly turned my thoughts back to days long gone by. "The Windham collection of paintings will be on exhibition every Monday and Thursday in the lower floor of the Town-Hall. Admission free."

Windham! No, I could not be mistaken; that was the name. A Windham had played the leading rôle in the

last chapter of my youthful romance.
Now, it dawned upon me that I had
heard later that this Windham
had settled down with
his young wife here in B—. Since
that time I had heard nothing of him.
And now, to be reminded of him, in
this unlooked-for way!

But you will not understand what
there was in a simple newspaper notice
to move me so strangely. I have to go
back still further.

You must know that as a younger
son of an Unter-Frankish family I was
educated in the Cadet-house at Munich,
and that in the year before the outbreak
of the Franco-Prussian War, I had acquired the rank of first-lieutenant. I
was twenty-nine years old, and had
had small experience of life outside of
my calling, to which I was devoted

body and soul.   A thoroughly ideal en-
sign love, which came to an absurd

end, had restrained me from the mani-
fold follies common to my age, but had
not given me the most exalted idea of
womanhood.  Still, I did not pose as a
woman-hater, and, as I was passion-
ately fond of dancing—a taste acquired
in the Military Academy—I took part
with the merriest in the Carnival of 1870,
but without burning my wings.

Until *my* hour struck also.   At one
of the public balls about the middle of
February appeared a striking young
beauty who eclipsed all previous society
queens.  She had but recently come

14

thither from Austria with her mother, to
seek social diversion for the winter,
having just laid off mourning for her
father whose death had occurred a year
before. Her form, her bearing, her
manner, all had a singular charm, which
was partly accounted for by the strange
mixture of her blood. Her mother, a
tall Scotch woman of strict puritanical deportment, had married a Styrian
nobleman who had fallen in love
with her while traveling through
her native Highlands. She returned with him to his estate, but had
never understood how to adapt herself
to new conditions. Nevertheless, she
had lived happily with her frivolous,
Romish husband, and had not yet overcome her grief at his death when she
set out to travel with her daughter.

The latter, who was at that time in
the early twenties, had until then seen
nothing of life save what was offered her
within a radius of ten miles of her estate.

The father, who had not been perhaps in all respects irreproachable, and who each year passed several months in Vienna, took care to keep his wife far from the temptations of the capital,

and to introduce no young gentlemen to his daughter. Both these precautions were, in fact, unnecessary, for they were by temperament cold and indifferent. In this very trait, Abigail—for so the daughter was named, in accordance with an ancient custom in her mother's family—was the true child of her mother, between whom and herself there was no outward resemblance, not even in the color of her hair.

But I will make no foolish attempt to

describe this charming young beauty. Two characteristics caught my attention at our first meeting and pursued me, even in my dreams : the strange, steady look of her great gray eyes, which always remained serious, even when the mouth smiled, and the rounded beauty of her arms, which I had never seen equaled. Contrary to the custom at that period she wore them quite bare, and only outlined from her queenly shoulders by a narrow band—a fashion which the ladies, especially the mothers, regarded as scandalous, albeit the Viennese mode sanctioned the costume ; and the Fräulein was, in speech and manner, quite irreproachable. But the arms were too fair to be kept covered, and naturally provoked as much envy as admiration. Their color was like that of creamy white satin, with a faint glow, and in the curves of the elbows a blue vein. Even the tiny white scar high upon the left arm had a peculiar charm, as if, with

17

intentional coquetry it had been imprinted upon the smooth skin, to set off to better advantage its exquisite fineness; and such a hand as was disclosed when she drew off her gloves at supper! such a dainty foot in its white satin shoe! An elegance and proportion for which she had to thank her Austrian blue blood, and not her Scottish Highland descent. With the first look that I cast upon that splendid creature, I succumbed to the witchery of her strange, cold eyes. Invulnerable as I had heretofore been to the charms of lovely women, my heart beat violently, and my speech was confused when I was presented to her and begged her for a dance. I did not even recover myself while whirling around the spacious salon, and was enraged that I should cut such an awkward figure. The thought was up-

permost : she is not like other women
—she is a goddess. No wonder that
her glance falls with such cold lustre
upon us poor children of men ! Is it
for one moment to be imagined
that such a mouth was meant
to be kissed ? and as for the
poor mortal who might dare
to throw his arm about her
neck, must not his reason for-
sake him and he be reduced
to a little heap of ashes by
this more than human happiness.

You see, it was a veritable enchantment. All that I had heard told

of sudden and violent attachments I
was now to experience. However, I
soon gained sufficient mastery over myself to submit to my fate with a good
grace, and was able on this first even-

ing to play the part of a chivalric ad-
mirer without allowing myself to be
drawn into any such extravagant hom-
age as the most of my comrades yielded
her. And this was of more advantage
to me than to have surpassed them all
in beauty and attractiveness. For this
singular girl, although it was her first
season in society, received all the at-
tentions which fell to her lot, as well as
the flattery of her partners in the dance,
with as much indifference as though it
had been the movement alone which
made dancing enjoyable, and the vain
young gentlemen, so finely trimmed and
attired, were only welcome as a means
to that end.

This she admitted to me quite inno-
cently as we were chatting together at
supper, and she confessed that she found
it tedious and tiresome to be continually
gazed upon and flattered because of her
beauty. No trace of coquetry could be
detected in her, but there was a tinge

of irony and contempt, which
in a less charming being
would have served to
·repel one, but in Fraü-
lein Abigail seemed only
a piece of adornment,
like a girdle of thorns
about the pliant form.

As I uttered no word of flattery we
became very good friends on this first
evening, and I even received from the
mother permission to call at her home.

As you may easily fancy, I availed
myself of it the following day. I had
naturally to inquire how they enjoyed
the ball, and I found the ladies in fur-
nished apartments, so luxuriously ap-
pointed that it was evident they were in
the most affluent circumstances. The
mother made no concealment of the
fact that she had come for the purpose
of finding a desirable husband for her
daughter—of which there was no pros-
pect at their country-seat. The girl

**heard** every remark which bore upon this subject with the utmost indifference, as if she were not herself personally interested, but regarded the whole affair as a whim of her mother's which **it** was **to be** hoped would **soon** disappear.

The confidence which she had thus early reposed in me, she **did** not again withdraw; on the contrary, she **gave** me continually new proofs that my presence was agreeable to **her,** that my way of looking at men and things in general seemed to her the right one. She told me freely about her past **life,** in which was little of romance. She had **never been in** love, and confided to me **that** her fancy could not conceive what such a state of the heart was like. The **only man** she had ever **been fond of had** been her father. Her **mother** she could **in no** wise understand, and she **performed all** filial duties mechanically, **as it** were, without the least feeling in the matter. " Yes," she said to me once, " perhaps it is as you say; I have not the same nature as other girls, and yet——" here she closed her eyes, leaned her beautiful blond head back, and her half-parted lips wore an expression of thirst and longing that was half pained, half wild. The next instant they broke into a smile, and she began a mocking discourse upon certain young ladies with whom she had become ac-             quainted and

who issued constant bulletins upon the condition of their tender hearts.

All these confidences were far from making me vain or arousing in me any false hopes. Almost every evening passed like the last, in the company of the two ladies—sometimes, while the Carnival lasted, at public fêtes, where I already passed for her inseparable cavalier and favored suitor—sometimes around their cosy tea-table, as the one family friend of my own sex. Now and then, when an elderly lady, an Austrian acquaintance of her mother, was present, there was a little farce played, at which Abigail was always a spectator. She did not conceal her *ennui*, as she concealed no other feeling, and still there was a dark abyss in her being, which sometimes disclosed itself, in an unguarded moment, and each time sent through me a slight shiver of uneasiness.

As the weeks and months went by, I became so communicative to her that I did not disguise this not very flattering feeling from my fair young friend. She stared calmly into space with eyes immovable.

"I know what you mean," she said. "There is something in me of which I myself am afraid, and I still can not define it more clearly. Perhaps it is a premonition that I shall never know what happiness means; and may, even without fault on my part, be destined to bring no happiness to others; and then my inmost being rises in protest and seeks something on which to avenge itself for this deprivation. Do you know how I seem to myself? Like an icicle which beholds a flame flicker merrily, and is ashamed that it remains so stiff and cold, and then bends

towards it, to gain nothing thereby, but only to melt slowly away; and when the last icy rigidity has vanished, its own very existence is at an end. The comparison is rather lame, I confess, but it is significant, and perhaps you know what is meant by the flame."

This was the first time she had alluded to my infatuation, which had for a long time been no secret. Ruthlessly enough she did it, surely cutting off all hope at one blow.

But who knows where the conversation would have drifted if her mother had not entered. It was truly a lame comparison, for the flame did not burn as the true fire of love should,

but had strange intervals of coolness and attempts at complete extinction.

In fact, it was only at its brightest when I enjoyed a tête-a-tête with this wonderful girl ; or when, in the gaily-lighted ball-room, I was dazzled by her full beauty. She never ceased to engage my thoughts, even when out of my sight ; indeed, only then could I think calmly about her, and then it was always with a puzzling feeling of aversion on my part, though I had nothing definite to reproach her with. Was it a sin not to love me or to have felt even the slightest aspiration of love—and that dark abyss, which was a horror

even to herself, might it not one day appear as the favorable background against which all bright joys should stand out with a heightened color and charm ?

Nevertheless, the fact remained, I wished I had never known the beautiful girl, who attracted me to her anew whenever I was near her, and threw my heart into a turmoil as if by magic. Only to imprint one kiss upon those ripe lips, to feel those slender, white arms embracing me! I pictured this to myself, and forthwith the spell was broken and I was restored to myself.

The mother saw me come and go without giving herself any special concern as to my relations with her daughter. That I was in love seemed to her only natural, but not at all dangerous in her daughter's present mental attitude, which she knew only too well, and did not seek to combat; for, with all her outward piety, she was possessed by the spirit of worldly speculation. She had higher ambitions for her popular daughter than my position as first-lieutenant could offer her; and she hoped, above all things, that through my acquaintance her entrance into aristocratic circles would be facilitated. Then, she calculated, there would be, in the long run, some Count for a son-in-law, or she might even tolerate a morganatic alliance.

The advent of summer interrupted her plans, for "society" dispersed and betook itself to the country. The two ladies rented a villa at Tegernsee, to my chagrin, for I could now visit them only once a week. This deprivation so heightened my ardor that the interval between the Saturdays was passed in feverish impatience, in constant anxiety, lest, in my absence, some one else might ingratiate himself with the two lonely ladies, who would satisfy the demands of the mother, and be not more unwelcome to the daughter than any other *parti*.

This anxiety was superfluous. Over the whole German land the air grew dark with a threatening cloud which threw into the shadow all individual affairs. The Franco-Prussian war broke out. I hailed it with joy, as likely to put an end to my own unendurable position. Only with great difficulty, and by undertaking a night's ride, could I afford the time for a parting visit to Tegernsee. Arriving in the early morning, I found the object of my devotion in the garden as she had not expected my coming. She was fresh from her bath, and the morning breeze played over her fair skin, and the blond hair, which fell like a soft mantle about her shoulders. When she heard what had brought me thither at such an unusual hour, she did not for an instant change color, but her eyelids drooped softly, as though she would let down a curtain before that which was passing in her mind.

"Well," she said "then your ardent wish will be fulfilled: you will perform miracles of valor, and will return a renowned conqueror. I wish you all success and shall think of you daily."

"Will you really do that?" I said, "and a trifle more tenderly than of every other mother's son who bares his brow and breast, *pro patria*, to the bullets of the French?"

"How can you doubt it?" she said, breaking off a flower and inhaling its fragrance with that same expression of longing. "You know that I am very fond of you, and that I confide in you more than in any other young

31

man of my acquaintance. **Are** you not content with that?"

"**No,** Abigail," I said, "and you **know very** well why." **And** now I poured **out for** the first time—thinking that perhaps it might be the last—all that I felt for her in one passionate outburst. "I know," I concluded, "you have not the same feeling. The lightning which has shattered my heart has not **so much as** singed one little curl upon **your** forehead. Moreover, I am not so blinded **as to** think that you would, **out** of sheer pity, feign a warmer feeling, rather than see me go away quite hopeless, into the field. Yet, for **my** own relief I must for once let my lips give utterance. And now, commend me to your mother, whose morning toilet I will not interrupt, and keep a kindly thought for me."

Then she raised her eyes and looked me full in the face, very earnestly, while the otherwise even color of her cheeks took on a faint blush which became her well.

"No," she said, "you must not go from me so, when God only knows

whether we shall ever see you again. I will make this admission to you : I am almost convinced that could you, for a few weeks or months longer, show yourself as kind and friendly to me as now, the conscious icicle would be transformed into a fresh green shoot, and burst into bloom. Another poor comparison, but you will understand me. Perhaps sometimes, when in the cold bivouac you are unable to sleep, you will think

**of this** Spring fairy-tale and let it warm your chilled heart."

I cannot describe what courage these words gave me. Heaven knows what **I** stammered out in the first rush **and** whirlwind of feeling; only from her response, which I remembered word for word, **I** must conclude that among other things **I** insisted that she go **to** her mother at once to ask **for** her blessing, and thus seal our understanding **as** a regular binding betrothal.

" If **you** are not satisfied with my **explanation**," she said coldly, " I am **sorry**; **but at** present, I do not feel disposed **to go** further." Yes, " disposed," was what she said, and withal, she looked charming and cool enough to drive one to distraction. " If we should **be** betrothed in due form I should not know an hour's peace, but should be forever supposing, like Bürger's Lenore, not merely **the** continued uncertainty :

34

are you faithless, William, or dead?—I should fear something even worse. I am frightfully superstitious; or, to go further, I believe fix-edly and firmly that that ballad is not a mere grewsome fable, but that in the main features such a thing really happened. If some mortal fate should befall you, dear friend, and you had a strong claim upon me, as upon your solemnly-betrothed bride, I should not sleep another night, and I know of a certainty that some apparition would put an end to my poor existence. So leave our future to the care of Heaven, and go forth into the field attended everywhere by my most affectionate thoughts."

This was intended to subdue my high-strung mood. In vain I tried in jest and in earnest, to move her, to induce her to grant me something more **definite.** Not even a promise that **she** would write to me, could I extract **from her,** and at last I had to tear myself away, with very conflicting emotions. There was no hint of true affection in the embrace which she suffered, rather than returned ; and the **lips** which I dared to touch lightly, **were** as cold **as** if they had not a moment before spoken words full **of** promise.

No **matter**; as a hopeless lover I had come, and as a happy, if not a declared bridegroom, I rode away.

My success had not indeed been overwhelming—it consisted only in this: In the moments when I was off duty I could think what a victor's prize awaited me upon the, then uncertain, termination of the war, providing she should feel " disposed " to reward my love and constancy; and that I was permitted to send, from time to time, assurances of this love and constancy, together with reports from the seat of war, to Tegensee, and later on, to Munich. No answer ever came. At first I felt no anxiety. Was it not perfectly correct that a young girl should write no tender letters to a young man to whom she had not been formally betrothed? And other than tender letters would not have made me happy. Moreover, who could tell whether the puritanical mamma who, it was probable, did not favor the relationship, had not interposed a decided prohibition? But all the mothers in the world, all considerations of propriety, could not have deterred a **truly loving** heart from sending a little comfort to a lover, far away, in the midst of privations and dangers. How I envied my comrades certain little notes, with which they stole away **to some** quiet corner where they could enjoy such "love-tokens" all undisturbed. I went empty-handed away from every post, to which however I, **on my** part, contributed more largely than many a more favored man. And one day I grew ashamed of the all-too-onesided part which I was playing. I resolved not to write another line until some inquiry was made for me. She might look upon me as "faithless or dead"—it remained for her to show whether my life or death had the slightest significance for her.

Weeks and months passed after this resolve, **and** no word came. Still, **if** you fancy that I suffered more keenly under this complete collapse of all my hopes, you deceive yourself. I experienced, rather, a certain relief, and realized that all the time I had been subject to deceptive illusion of happiness and love, since, in reality, only my mind had been in the game, and possibly beside this, there had been a secret determination to approach still closer to this unapproachable being, and to melt the ice.

What had happened to me gave me in good season a wholesome lesson. She would not have been the wife I needed. It was fortunate that I could withdraw with a good conscience, and remain stationary where I then stood, without knowing that she even wished to approach me by a single step.

So the year drew to a close; we had exchanged neither Christmas nor New Year greetings. In February I received a wound, and was transport-

ed to Mainz. It does not belong here
to tell how, in that house in which
through long weeks I received the most

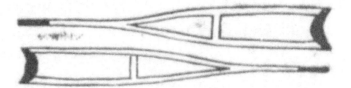

loving care, I met her who the following year became my wife. The word
which decided our fate had not yet been
spoken; we only knew that we belonged
to each other for life, when one day there
came a letter from Abigail. She had
read in the newspaper that I had been
wounded and would ask whether I in
anywise needed her help—whether she
and her mother should come and nurse
me. Of any deep feeling there was no
trace—a letter whose con-
tents might have pro-
ceeded from the imper-
sonal demands of com-
mon benevolence.

Perchance the mother

had dictated it. But need **the daughter** have copied it thus slavishly?

**I** bade Helen—whom I then first **told of my now** severed relation—return thanks **in** my name for the kind offer; but I was in want of nothing and had the best of care.

That was the last sign of life which I received from my "graven image" **whom I** had worshipped. The last of all **was my** marriage announcement, sent out by me **in** the **autumn** of '71, and which came back from Munich without having been delivered.

When I returned home myself, a short time after, I learned that before **the** entry of the victorious troops the ladies had departed, **no** one knew whither; possibly they had returned to their country-seat in Austria.

At all events, in **the** following year the report reached us that the fair Abigail had married a wealthy resident of northern Germany, a man well **on in** years, whom she had met at a watering place. Further, that he was a fine man, universally esteemed, a great lover of art, and the owner of a choice collection of the modern masters; that he had appropriated the fair Fräulein rather as an ornament to his gallery, a plastic work of art—for he was thirty-five years her senior, and tormented with serious gouty infirmities.

That the *cold fish*, as Abigail was sometimes dubbed, had not hesitated long before entering upon such an alliance, no one seemed to question.

Since that I had never heard a word from her; even the name of the place where she lived had escaped my memory, which retained only her name —Windham. And now I read it all unexpectedly in the local paper, and could not doubt that it was her husband whose picture gallery was here mentioned. I summoned the waiter and asked if he could tell me any particulars concerning the owner of this gallery and his family.  He knew nothing further than that Mr. Windham had died several years before, and had bequeathed his collection to the State. Whether he left a wife he could not say. Perhaps the proprietor would know. He, however, was sitting with a couple of friends at cards in his private room and did not like to be disturbed. I, too, forbade such an interruption also, and sought to persuade

**myself** that it was **not of** the slightest interest to me whether a certain Frau Abigail Windham lived as a widow in this town, or somewhere with her mother upon their Styrian estate. An image, a name—and perchance in these eleven years the original had faded or grown dim, and a meeting would not be desirable for either of us.

**Let** me admit that a certain sense of **guilt, never** quite suppressed, stirred again within me. On the whole, what **had I to** reproach her with? She had simply **not** kept what she had never promised to keep; and it had been my own folly to expect of her what nature **had** denied her.

**Who** knows; if I had relied upon **her** simple **word,** and had entrusted **everything to** the future, would not the tender stalk of her inclination toward me, have, in the end, thriven and blossomed. And a heart so long closed, would have had more of

worth in it than one which opens
itself in a day. No, it had been base
fickleness to turn so suddenly from her.
Of course, as to whether I would have
been as happy with her as with my
Helen! But that had nothing to do
with it. I had boasted of my own
fidelity. And, if there had been undue
haste, I, as a man of honor, was bound
to redeem myself.

Similar considerations had forced
themselves upon me more than once in
the course of the last few years, and
had always been parried with sophisms.
That evening they gained such a power-
ful hold upon me that I sat there in a
very troubled mood, a bitter taste upon
my tongue, which even the excellent
wine could not obliterate.

And so it had grown late. The players had left the place, only a solitary chess party continued stubbornly. At last I rose to depart, and noticed for the first time that heavy wine and heavy thoughts do not go well together; for my head was burning, and I felt a grave pressure upon my heart. This grew somewhat better as I stepped out into the cool night air, and took my well-known way to the inn; I did not meet a living soul, save the night watchman, who, in this ancient town, still made the rounds with pike and lantern. The lantern was superfluous, for a bewitching moonlight lay upon roof and pavement, and showed in bright relief the intricate carving upon the old balconies and even the inscriptions above the house

doors.   The night was so wonderful
that I even made a detour before I concluded to seek my room, which had
been rather sultry during the day.   It
was to be hoped the chambermaid had
left the windows open.

And so I reached the hotel, found
the door yet ajar, and the porter in his
crèche sunk in profound slumber.   I did
not grudge him his rest,
especially as I had
hidden the room-
key.   The way up
the stairs I could find
without a guide, by
the aid of a drowsy
gaslight.   I hoped to
have a good sleep, for
I felt a leaden weariness in every
limb.   But when I opened the door
I saw something which dispelled all my
dreamy dullness and riveted me, with
an exclamation of astonishment, to the
threshold.

The two windows of the room over-looked an open square and admitted a broad flood of moonlight. This only emphasized the darkness of the further corner of the room, where against the wall stood a sofa. And, yet, I saw plainly that some one was sitting on the sofa—a dark-robed female figure, with nothing light about her, save the face. That looked forth immovably from be-neath a black veil which was held to-gether under the chin with one hand, while the other hand held a bunch of flowers up to the face. She must have taken it from the glass which stood upon the table by the sofa; a couple of roses and a spray of jasmine which the wife of my friend had gathered in her garden after dinner.

Even at my entrance this veiled figure did not stir in the least. As soon as I gained courage and stepped softly to the table—words failed, I could not trust my eyes—the stranger raised her head, which she had suffered to lie back against the sofa, and I saw now quite plainly, despite the darkness, two great gray eyes fastened upon me.

" Abigail ? "

The figure remained quietly seated, she seemed not in the least embarrassed; only she let the hand that held the flowers sink in her lap. Then, after a little, I heard her say—the voice sounded weird and strange to me:

" Do you really know me again? Has all the trouble which you have given yourself to forget me been in vain? Well, all the more honor to you! I see that, at any rate, I have estimated you rightly."

" Abigail ! " I cried again. " Is it possible? You here? How came you in this room at this untimely hour ? "

I had now grown accustomed to the
semi-darkness, and saw plainly that her
mouth was slightly drawn; otherwise,
she seemed to me fairer even than my
remembrance of her, only paler, and
with the brows at times contracted as
if from pain.

"How did I come here?" she repeated, slowly, with a slight hoarse-
ness in her voice, as of one who living
alone is often silent the day long.
That is very simple. I heard you were
here for a short time. That you would
not hunt me up, I knew well enough;
and so there was nothing for me but to
come to you myself. To be sure, no
one showed me the way up here; the
porter was asleep. But I read your name
upon the black tablet downstairs, and
against it the number of
your room; so I
made so free as to
settle myself comfort-
ably here to await you.

50

I so longed in my loneliness—my **hus-**band died three years ago—to see **once** more an old friend. As you know, *on revient toujours*. To be sure, such a poor *revenant* cuts but a sorry figure : but if I have grown ugly, you need not reproach me with it. Yours is the blame—but of that we will not talk now. One should not spoil the bliss of the present with unlovely retrospect."

Still, I could not find a word to reply. What to make of the whole matter was a problem to me. Abigail, whom I had known as proud and reserved, now **here** at midnight to greet me again !

" It is so dark here," I stammered at last ; "allow me to strike a light."

" No, do not," she interrupted. " It **is** light enough to look into each other's **eye**s, and what need we further ? I am **vain**, you should know, and you must **not** see upon my face the traces of the **years** that have elapsed since our last meeting. **I have** not passed the time altogether merrily. If you had not left **me** I should perhaps have been con- **tent; and** she who feels herself happy **does** not grow old."

"Gracious lady!" I cried, and would fain have told her that, though I did not feel myself entirely free from fault, she had been partly responsible for what had occurred.

"Call me by my maiden name, and **not** 'gracious lady!'" she interposed. **"As** long **as** my husband was living **I had to** submit to this style of address, **which ill** suited me. I was only the tender-hearted sister of a good man— **not his wife.** Nay, and something **more** than a sister; his model, which **he deified,** worshipped, whose beauty **he was never** tired of praising. At first **this** gave me pleasure; but soon I grew **weary** of it, and to have him draw me **in a** hundred attitudes and poses seemed to me but **an** intolerable bore.

Yet what was I to do? It was his only joy—of that I could not deprive him, he was such a good, noble man; far better than you. And yet I felt as though I were emancipated when at last he succumbed beneath his sufferings."

"Abigail," I said, " I am glad that I can at last roll from my heart the burden which has so long oppressed it "— and then I told her everything; my grief over her coldness, the disappointed hope that, during the long campaign, the bands about her heart would loosen; and how, at last, I despaired of ever melting the ice in which it seemed incased.

"Oh!" she said, with a slight trembling of the voice, "you place too much to your credit, my fine sir. If you had really loved me, your patience would not have been exhausted by waiting until I, who must needs learn painfully to spell out love, should at last arrive at Z. But as soon as you were once in the field, I ceased to exist for you."

"How can you say that! All those letters that I wrote."

"I never received a single one."

We stared at each other; upon each the same thought thrust itself—her mother had intercepted my letters. But with neither of us did it pass the lips.

"Ah, well!" she said at last, "what is the use of breaking one's head, or worse, one's heart, over that which is lost. You found a satisfactory substitute, and with me even, things might have been worse. I confess to you frankly, I do not know myself sometimes, whether at heart I am good or evil. Perhaps I am neither; perhaps

nature feels that
when she has en-
dowed a being
with unusual beauty, she has done
enough for him, and need bestow
upon him nothing further in life. My
husband, too, who was an art enthusiast,
desired nothing more. But you, I
fancy, would soon have wearied of
admiring my beautiful arms and
shoulders."

At this she flung aside her black veil,
and leaned back, half-reclining in the
most charming attitude, surveying herself gravely, but without vanity, as one
might regard a statue. She had in
fact grown more beautiful with maturity,
the white arms a trifle fuller, and even
now there was only over the shoulders
a narrow band that threatened every
instant to slip off, whereupon she calmly
pushed it up into place again. I saw
once more the three tiny scars on the
left arm, and once more I longed to

press my lips upon her arms and to feel them like smooth, soft serpents entwined about my neck. At last, as though grown restless under my penetrating gaze, she drew the folds of her veil together across her bosom, and rose.

"This little nosegay I will take as a memento," she said. "You have far more beautiful flowers than we; and they are fragrant, which ours are not."

She drew forth a handful of immortelles which she had worn in the low corsage of her black satin gown.

"Will you have them—also for a memento? For whom should I adorn myself, if not for a dear friend? Every day is not like this one to me."

"Abigail," I cried, now

aroused, as in her full beauty she stood before me in the moonlight, her **blond** hair shining beneath her veil, **" is this** to be our last meeting? You are **now** free, and I am as lonely **as** you; **and** that we could not come together before we now see was not our fault. Dear Abigail, **can** you—can you still consent to be my wife."

I sprang toward her and would have caught her in my arms, but she drew a long step backward and stretched **out** both hands warningly.

" No, my good **sir !** " she said, **and** the **cool,** mocking expression **of the** white **face** checked my ardor. **" Don't** let us be foolish. You have **given me** to understand what life can **be at the** side of a beloved being. **That can never be** repeated. You **would be making** constant comparisons **between** me **and** the good little woman who made you so happy and was so very different from me. Can you deny that, in your opinion, a better wife no man ever had? Well, suppose I had wished that my husband had been thirty years younger. No one will ever worship me as he worshipped me. So, a truce to all this, and no more sighs and lamentations! But I see plainly that you are in love with me, and why should I let you pine away? I am not my own mistress; and if one has failed to drink the cup of happiness, why should one hesitate to create at least a brief illusion of bliss, when the thirsty soul needs refreshing?"

I cannot describe how strangely these words affected me—this tone of mingled seriousness and frivolity, of resignation and defiance was so strange in this being once so cool and reserved.

I heard her laugh softly. "You wonder that in spite of my puritanical training I am so little of a prude. Well, that passes away with years; and the dark abyss yawns nearer: from rage and chagrin over a lost life, even an angel might grow into a devil. But have no fear, I will not thrust myself upon you—I, a poor *revenant*, could not harm you. So, fare you well, and good-night!"

She had spoken these words with such a peculiar, muffled voice, as of one resigned to some sad fate, that my whole heart responded to her. I stretched out my arms to draw her to my breast, but again she drew back.

"Not here," she whispered; "at my home, no cock crows when society pays me a visit. Follow me! Let us lose no more time: the hours hasten, and happiness flies with them."

She turned toward the door, and I saw again with enchantment, her light, swaying movement, as she glided noiselessly across the carpet. My head was confused as I followed her downstairs, where the gas was now extinguished, and out of the unguarded

house. Once
would have
her with my
shook her
and went
way, yet so
to me that
toward me
breath touch-
did not hap-
For the most
only her pro-
thirsty look
half open, so
gleamed
the upper lip
slightly. She
her head
hair, .which
bound, fell
shoulders
mered be-

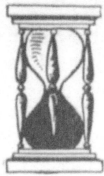

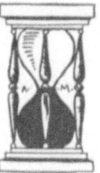

outside I
supported
arm; but she
head mutely,
calmly on her
close was she
as she turned
her cool
ed me. This
pen often.
part I saw
file, and the
of the mouth,
that the teeth
within, and
protruded
had thrown
back, and her
was un-
down on her
and shim-
neath the

veil. Her arms were folded upon
each other below her bosom, which

was bare, and the prey of the night winds.

"Are you not freezing?" I said. She only shook her head again, and cast upon me, suddenly, a side-long glance of suspicion.

"You feel embarrassed to walk the street with me in this attire. But be not alarmed, I have an unsullied reputation; no one would dare to assail it. Every one knows that I live quietly and discreetly, and the only man who ever crosses my threshold is the gardener, who keeps my flowers in order. Moreover, I never go out into the air. Why should I? To-day, I have made an exception on your account — *on revient toujours à ses premières amours;* but I have already said that before; when one loves one repeats oneself—and what if he does? You will not despise me for that."

Just at that instant a belated night - reveller came toward us, and passed us as if he saw only me, and not the beautiful, strangely-dressed woman at my side, whose handsome arms and shoulders gleamed white beneath her veil. I heard her laugh softly. "Did I not tell you? only he has good taste not to make me feel embarrassed. But what does it matter! Whose affair is it if I choose the company of an old friend, although he has not deserved so well of me?" As noiselessly as though her feet were bare, and as she spoke she hurried forward so rapidly that I could scarcely keep pace with her.

Then we came in front of a gateway. The neighborhood was entirely unfamiliar to me; some shabby houses, in which workmen might have lived, stood on each side of the dusty road planted with poplars, and at last every trace of a settlement ceased. The moon had gone behind a bank of dark clouds, the wind had risen and whistled through the dry branches above our heads. "Are we almost there?" I asked, as a feeling of uneasiness oppressed me more and more. "Almost," she whispered. "You can already see the wall of my garden, there to the left. My dwelling lies within it. But you are tired! Do you wish to turn back?"

Instead of answering I sought to draw her to me. But she evaded me.

"Wait!" she said. "Here we are already. You will be surprised to see how prettily I live."

We stood before a broad iron grating

which closed the entrance to a large garden. All that was to be seen of the park was an avenue stretching far into the distance, and formed of yews and cypresses, between which marble statues shone out here and there. At the extreme end rose a one-storied structure with a dome-like roof. But the sky was so overcast that at this distance I could discern nothing distinctly.

"Will you not unlock the gate?" I asked. "The night is passing."

"Oh, it is long enough," she answered softly, in a scornful tone, "and I have forgotten the key. "What shall we do now?"

"There is a bell at the side of the

wicket," I said. "It will waken the gardener if he is asleep."

" Do not trouble yourself to pull the bell! No one must know that I admit you—the old man least of all. He would hold me in contempt, and never water my flowers again. But we need no one. If we bend ourselves a little the thing is easily done."

As she said this, I saw her glide through the space between the palings as easily as though, instead of her woman's figure, a cloud had floated through.

And now she stood on the other side, holding fast to the railing with both hands. " Who loves me will follow me! " she cried again with her malicious laugh; but at the same time her rich beauty shone full upon me.

" Do not play with me so cruelly! " I cried. " You see well enough that I cannot come to you in that fashion. You have lured me so far, now pray get the key and let me in!"

"That would suit the gentleman well, no doubt!" she mocked, through the grating, and her eyes flashed. "But when the cocks crow you would leave me alone again, for I am only beautiful by night. When the sun shines I dare not let myself be seen. No, fine sir, it was only that you might give me a safe escort hither, for a timid woman does not like to be alone on the streets at midnight. And now, with

thanks for the knightly service, I wish the Herr Major, or whatever his title may be, a pleasant journey."

She made a low courtesy, in which her figure showed more graceful than ever, and turned slowly away to walk down the avenue.

"Abigail!" I cried, beside myself., "is it possible you can treat me so inhumanly—to show me first all Heaven open, and then plunge me pitilessly in the Hell of your scorn? If I have forfeited the right ever to call you mine, at least do not drive me from you in despair. Give me one drop of love to taste, one kiss, Abigail! Not as on that day when your heart was not upon your lips, but as one might kiss a friend in whom one had pardoned a great transgression!"

She stopped and turned slowly round toward me. "If the gentleman is served with so little," she said, "Abigail is not cruel, even though Life has played cruelly with her."

She turned about and came back, close up to the grating. With both her smooth, white arms she reached through the bars and drew my head quickly to her face, quite close; I saw her great gray eyes, which shone with a cold brilliancy, without love, and without hate. Then I felt her lips pressed to mine, and a strange shudder, half of fear, half of bliss, ran through my blood. Her lips were cold, but her breath scorched me, and it seemed as though she drew my very soul from my body. All grew black before my eyes; my breath left me. I struggled in terror to free myself, but her cool, white lips remained firmly pressed upon mine. Then I strove to extricate myself from the embrace of her arms—the soft serpents wound about my neck like hoops of steel. Where was the strength of my arms? It was as if their very marrow had been consumed by that kiss; they fell power-less at my side; the sweat of death stood on my forehead; like some poor, helpless sinner, tortured upon the rack, I hung at that grating. I would fain have screamed, but no tone could force its way through those fast-closed lips; thoughts rushed through my brain, as of one who is sinking in the deep sea; ten minutes more of this torment and it would have been all over with me. Then a sound like the cracking of a whip broke in upon the awful stillness, and instantly the mouth loosened from mine, a peal of laughter rang out from behind the bars, I lost consciousness and fell in a swoon.

When I came to myself again, I saw my friend the doctor kneeling beside

me, busied in rubbing my forehead and temples with some fluid which he took  from his medicine case. His carriage stood near by in the avenue; I understood that it was to his coachman I owed my deliverance from the ghost, whom the snapping of his whip had frightened away.

"What the devil, old friend, are you looking for out here in the graveyard at the ghost-hour!" exclaimed the doctor, when he had revived me a little, and I was able, with his support, to totter toward the carriage. "You are trembling in every limb, your lips are bleeding—if you thought this would be a proper supplement to your cure at Wildbad, to sleep here, out in the night dew, upon the cold earth, you were greatly mistaken."

Not for the world would I have told him the real situation. The fiery wine had driven me out thus late, I said, and I had at last come to the gate where I had meant to rest a moment, but had been overcome by giddiness, and had fallen to the ground. This did not sound improbable. Moreover, after my helpful friend had put me to bed at my hotel, I fell at once into a sound, deep sleep, in which I needed no anxious watcher. When I rose late in the morning, cheered by a visit from the doctor, every trace of my uncanny night-visitor seemed to have disappeared.

Still, I was by no means as brave as was befitting a soldier, and when evening came—the day I had spent in my room, brooding over the occurrence — I wrote my friend a note to the effect that I was obliged to leave on the night train. Even then I did not give the real reason; a physician,—a skeptic by vocation,—how could I think that he would give credence to my report? Had I not reason to fear that I should seem to him either a singular fanatic, or a fanciful dreamer? But mine was a dream which left visible traces in reality. When I went to my table in the morning, the nosegay of roses and jasmine had disappeared from the glass; while upon the sofa lay a dry little cluster of faded immortelles.